Magic Animal Friends

For Elsie, with love
'All the stars in the night sky'

Special thanks to Valerie Wilding

ORCHARD BOOKS

First published in Great Britain in 2015 by Orchard Books
This edition published in 2018 by The Watts Publishing Group

5 7 9 10 8 6

A CIP catalogue record for this book is available from the British Library.

ISBN 978 1 40834 848 2

Printed in Great Britain by Clays Ltd, Elcograf S.p.A.

FSC www.fsc.org MIX Paper from responsible sources FSC® C104740

The paper and board used in this book are made from wood from responsible sources

Orchard Books

An imprint of Hachette Children's Group
Part of The Watts Publishing Group Limited
Carmelite House, 50 Victoria Embankment, London EC4Y 0DZ

An Hachette UK Company

www.hachette.co.uk

www.hachettechildrens.co.uk

Ruby Fuzzybrush's Star Dance

Daisy Meadows

ORCHARD

Shining House
Sunshine Meadow
Blossom Briar
Goldie's Grotto
Toadstool Cafe
Toadstool Glade
Mrs Taptree's Library
Library
Friendship Tree
Maze
Silver Spring
Buttercup Grove
Lighthouse

Map of Friendship Forest
Ace Air Travel
Windmill
Mr Cleverfeather's Inventing Shed
Muddlepups' Den
Treasure Tree
Sparkly Falls
Featherbills' Barge
Waterwheel
Entrance to the Caverns
Swamp
Grizelda's Tower

Can you keep a secret? I thought you could!
Then I'll tell you about an enchanted wood.
It lies through the door in the old oak tree,
Let's go there now - just follow me!
We'll find adventure that never ends,
And meet the Magic Animal Friends!

Love

Goldie the Cat

Contents

CHAPTER ONE

Sunset in the Forest

As it got dark, Lily Hart and her best friend, Jess Forester, grinned at each other excitedly. They'd been waiting all day for the sun to go down, so that some very special animals would wake up! As they left the barn, the last of the sunshine lit up the sign on the door: Helping Paw

Wildlife Hospital. Lily's parents had set up the hospital to look after all kinds of animals, and Lily and Jess helped out there whenever they could.

"I'm so excited," Jess said, twirling one of her blonde curls around her finger. "I've never fed a fox cub before."

"Me neither!" said Lily. "Wait until you see them, they're adorable!"

"You forgot these!" Mrs Hart popped out of the hospital and handed them each a feeding bottle full of milk and a torch. "Here you are," she said. "Have fun!"

Lily took Jess over to one of the special

runs her dad had made to keep the animal patients safe. It had a lid made of wire netting on a wooden frame. As Lily lifted it, two fluffy little faces with pointed noses and amber eyes peeped sleepily out from a wooden shelter.

"They're so cute!" exclaimed Jess.

"A lady from the village found them all alone yesterday afternoon," Lily said, shaking her head so that her dark bobbed hair swung around her face. "Dad said foxes are nocturnal, so they're supposed to sleep during the day and be awake at night-time."

The girls knelt down next to the run. The cubs tottered over on wobbly legs, with their long fluffy tails trailing in the grass. Soon they were guzzling

greedily on the warm milk.

When the bottles were empty, Jess and Lily replaced the wire cover. The sun was going down, but the cubs were wide awake. Lily and Jess turned on their torches and stayed to watch as the cute little fox cubs played with each other.

As she looked at them, Lily caught sight of something else glowing in the torchlight. Two shining eyes! Something was crouched underneath a nearby bush.

"Look, Jess," she whispered. "Maybe it's another fox cub."

As she spoke, the creature appeared.

"Even better – it's Goldie!" Lily gasped in delight.

A beautiful golden cat bounded over and curled around their legs.

The girls shared a wonderful secret with the little cat – she lived in Friendship Forest, a hidden world where all the animals could talk! Now, both girls were smiling with excitement.

"If Goldie's here, that means we're going back to Friendship Forest!" cried Jess happily.

"A night-time adventure with our animal friends!" Lily grinned in delight.

The cat immediately turned towards Brightley Stream, which ran across the bottom of the Harts' garden. Using the beams from their torches, Jess and Lily

followed Goldie over the stepping stones and into Brightley Meadow.

Lily shone her torch on a lifeless old oak tree in the middle of the meadow – the Friendship Tree. She glanced at Jess excitedly, knowing what would happen as they drew near.

Sure enough, the old tree burst into life. As leaves sprouted from every twig, a nightingale sang sweetly from the topmost branch

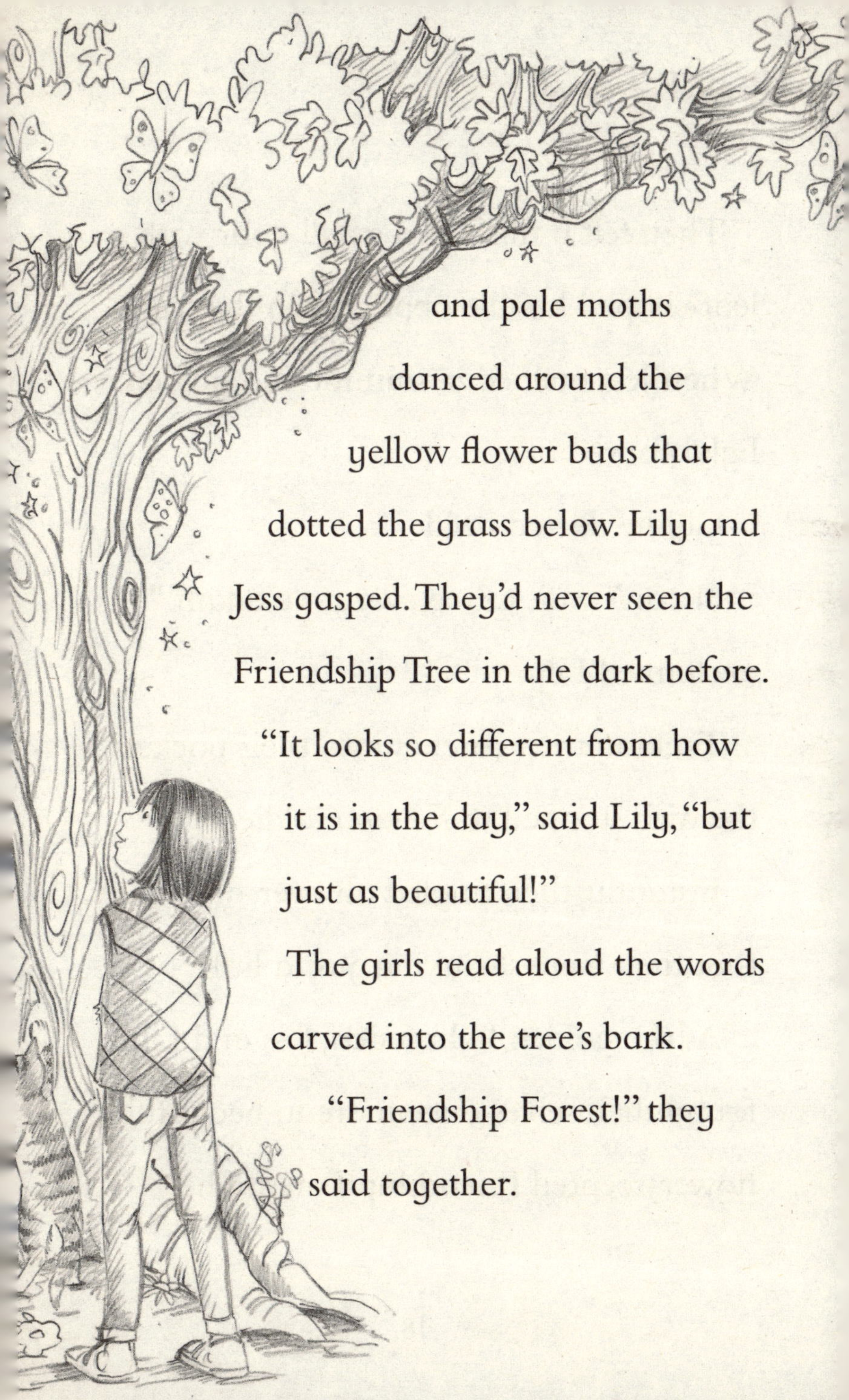

and pale moths danced around the yellow flower buds that dotted the grass below. Lily and Jess gasped. They'd never seen the Friendship Tree in the dark before.

"It looks so different from how it is in the day," said Lily, "but just as beautiful!"

The girls read aloud the words carved into the tree's bark.

"Friendship Forest!" they said together.

They felt a thrill as a small door with a leaf-shaped handle appeared in the trunk. When Jess opened it, shimmering golden light poured out.

Goldie darted inside.

"I can't wait to see everyone again!" exclaimed Lily.

Tucking their torches into their pockets, the girls stooped to follow Goldie.

Instantly, they tingled all over, and knew that they were shrinking, just a little.

As the golden light faded, Jess and Lily found themselves once more in beautiful, flower-scented Friendship Forest. The sun was setting here, too, casting long shadows, and the flowers were closing up for the evening.

Lily looked back. "The Friendship Tree's leaves aren't golden any more," she said in surprise. "They're turning silver!"

"That's because it's nearly night-time," said a soft voice.

The girls spun around. "Goldie!" they

cried, rushing to hug her.

The green-eyed cat was standing upright, wearing her golden scarf. As the girls were smaller, Goldie almost reached up to their shoulders, and now they were in Friendship Forest, she could talk!

"It's so lovely to see you," Jess told their friend. Then she noticed that Goldie's tail was twitching anxiously. "What is it, Goldie? Are Grizelda's dragons causing trouble again?"

Grizelda was an evil witch who wanted to make the animals leave Friendship Forest so she could have it all for herself.

The girls had managed to stop her wicked plans so far, but now she had dragons helping her!

Goldie sighed. "I think one of the dragons must be up to something. The Fuzzybrush fox family say they've seen strange things in the sky."

The girls stared at Goldie in dismay.

"It sounds like Grizelda's got a horrid new plan," said Lily.

"Whatever it is," said Jess fiercely, "we'll stop her. We won't let her or her dragons hurt Friendship Forest, Goldie – we promise!"

CHAPTER TWO

The Magical Moonstone

The setting sun streaked the sky above Friendship Forest with pinks and reds. As they walked through the forest, Lily waved to some blue tits who were snuggling down for the night in their nest in a hollow tree.

"Good night!" chirruped the smallest blue tit, yawning sleepily.

"Sleep well!" Jess called to the cute little birds.

"Everyone's going to bed!" Lily said.

"Not everyone!" Goldie said with a smile. "There are lots of nocturnal animals in Friendship Forest. Like the Fuzzybrush fox family."

"We'd better talk to them about the strange things they saw," Jess said.

"Where do they live?" Lily asked.

The cat smiled. "In a very unusual home," she said. "You'll see!"

After a while, a tall, narrow building came into view. Soft light glowed from the circular window at the top.

"It's a lighthouse!" cried Jess. "An orange and white striped lighthouse!"

"The Fuzzybrushes keep the lighthouse nightlight on when it's dark." Goldie explained. "With that and the stars, all the night-time animals can see their way around the forest,"

"Wow," breathed Lily. "Do you think the Fuzzybrushes would let us see inside?"

Before Goldie could reply, a door on the side of the lighthouse opened and the Fuzzybrush family ran out to meet them. Two larger foxes and two cubs bounded around the girls in a whirl of pointed noses, orange fur and fluffy tails.

"Welcome to our home," said Mrs Fuzzybrush proudly.

The adorable fox cubs bounded excitedly around the girls. The girl cub had a pretty bow around her neck, and the boy had a baseball cap on.

"Do you remember us?" the girl fox asked eagerly.

"Of course we do, Ruby," said Lily. "And you too, Rusty!" She gave them each a big hug.

The brave cubs had helped Goldie and the girls defeat Grizelda in their adventure with little Bella Tabbypaw the kitten.

"Could you tell us about the thing you saw in the sky?" Goldie asked Mr and Mrs Fuzzybrush.

"It was a black shadow, as big as me," said Mr Fuzzybrush in a gruff voice, "and it glided over the forest."

"It was spooky!" said Ruby. Rusty nodded in agreement.

The girls and Goldie exchanged glances. "This must be something to do with Grizelda," Lily whispered.

Mrs Fuzzybrush glanced up at the darkening sky. "The sun's almost set, children," she called, "so it's—"

"Star dance time!" cried Ruby.

Jess was puzzled. "What's a star dance?" she asked.

"Come with us," said Mr Fuzzybrush kindly, "and we'll show you!"

Everyone followed him inside the lighthouse. On the ground floor were a comfortable sitting room and three cosy bedrooms.

"That one's mine!" said Ruby proudly, as they passed a pretty round room decorated in red and pink.

"It's the colour of rubies!" said Lily.

Rusty rushed them past his bedroom.

"Mine's a bit untidy," he said.

The girls peeked inside and smiled as they saw a building set and little toy foxes scattered messily all over the bedroom floor.

They went up a spiral staircase right to the very top of the lighthouse. In the middle of the floor was a wooden star-shaped table.

Sitting on top of it was a smooth white stone,

the size of a watermelon. It glowed with a soft, pretty light.

"That's so beautiful," breathed Lily. "What is it?"

"It's the magical moonstone," Mr Fuzzybrush explained. "We need it for our star dance. Every evening we dance around it, to wake the stars. Then at dawn, we dance again to put them back to sleep."

"The star dance is a special dance that only foxes know," said Goldie. "It takes a really long time to learn."

"It's getting dark now," said Mrs

Fuzzybrush, "which means it's time for our star dance! Come on, children, let's go to the clearing!"

Mrs Fuzzybrush carefully picked up the moonstone and raced down the spiral staircase.

Lily and Jess followed the foxes as they hurried into a clearing next to the lighthouse. Mrs Fuzzybrush put the magical moonstone down in the centre and gave it a brush with her tail.

Ruby tugged at Lily's skirt. "Rusty and I know all the steps now!"

The Fuzzybrushes took up their

positions around the magical moonstone and began to dance.

Goldie, Jess and Lily watched in delight. The foxes stepped, dipped, glided and turned around the moonstone, weaving complicated patterns. Each time they swept past each other and their bushy tails touched, the glow from the moonstone grew brighter.

Lily glanced up at the night sky. "Look, Jess!" she whispered. "The stars are coming out."

Jess gazed at the sky. "It's so beautiful!" she cried. "Oh! The brighter the moonstone becomes, the more stars appear."

The girls stared in delight as hundreds – no, thousands – of stars winked and blinked in the darkness. Soon it was almost as bright as daytime, the forest lit up with sparkling silver starlight.

Suddenly, Rusty cried out, "Look, Mum, Dad! Up there in the sky!"

Everyone stopped dancing and turned to stare.

A dark shadow, just as Mr Fuzzybrush had described, was flying through the night sky.

Jess and Lily stared as it came closer.

"That's not a shadow," Lily said shakily.

"You're right," cried Jess. "It's one of Grizelda's dragons!"

CHAPTER THREE

Smudge the Dragon

The black dragon zoomed closer.

"He's heading straight towards the lighthouse!" cried Jess.

As he flew, the dragon's long scaly tail tangled around his back legs. He beat his black wings harder as he tried to swerve aside, but it was too late.

Crash! He bashed into the lighthouse roof and skidded on the tiles.

Ruby scooped up the moonstone and the foxes ran towards their home, followed by Goldie and the girls. As they got to the lighthouse, everyone gasped.

Long curved claws scrabbled at the roof. A cloud of soot puffed over the lighthouse, blocking out the nightlight that shone through the windows. Immediately, the forest went darker. The dragon scrambled over the roof and Ruby ducked as a tile crashed down.

The dragon peered down at the foxes.

Then he took off from the roof and circled around, lower and lower, until his tail caught around his wing and he bump-bump-bumped to the ground, sending up another puff of soot.

"He's so clumsy!" said Lily.

"And dirty!" said Goldie. She pointed to

the lighthouse, which was smeared with black soot. "What a mess! Grizelda called him Smudge, remember? No wonder!"

Smudge spotted something and grinned. Then he shook his wing free from his tail and swooped down towards Ruby Fuzzybrush.

"*Raargh!*" he roared, as he grabbed the magical moonstone out of her paws.

Jess heard Ruby start to cry and knelt down to stroke the

cub's soft, furry head.

"No more nightlight and no more stars," Smudge laughed. "The night should be the darkest dark."

Mr Fuzzybrush folded his paws crossly. "Now give that back," he said to Smudge. "We need the moonstone to make starlight so all the night-time animals can find their way."

Smudge stumbled over his tail as he landed and waddled over to Mr Fuzzybrush. "Grizelda wants the forest to be dark, and so do I," he said. "So there!" He took a deep breath, and huffed a great sooty cloud all over the foxes.

Lily and Jess expected them to start coughing. But they didn't. When the sooty cloud cleared, Mr and Mrs Fuzzybrush and Rusty had completely vanished!

"Hee hee!" Smudge giggled. He flapped his wings and took off. There was a sound of snapping branches as he crashed through the trees on his way back up into the night sky.

Beside Jess, Ruby stared in horror at the place where her family had been. "Mum! Dad! Rusty! They've disappeared!" she cried. "Where are they?"

"I don't know," said Jess, looking around desperately.

"Oh no!" cried Lily. "The stars are disappearing, too!"

"The moonstone!" Ruby wailed. "The stars are fading because Smudge has got the moonstone and we didn't finish the dance!" The little fox cub sniffled miserably. Then her eyes widened. "What's that?"

Lily and Jess looked, and groaned.

A familiar yellow-green orb was flying towards them. With a *cra-ack!* it exploded in a huge shower of nasty-smelling, yellow-green sparks and Grizelda appeared. Her long green hair snaked around her thin, bony face.

"Grizelda!" said Jess. "What's Smudge done to the Fuzzybrushes? Tell him to bring them back right now!"

The witch threw back her cloak, revealing her shiny purple tunic and tight trousers, and her pointy-toed boots.

"Ha haaa!" she cackled. "No more starlight! The night-time animals will get lost and fall down holes and bump into things, because they won't be able to see. Then they'll have to leave the forest! Ha ha haaa!"

The girls glared at her. Ruby hid behind Jess's legs.

"That's not all," Grizelda said gleefully. "No more starlight means no more Friendship Tree."

"What?" gasped Lily.

"Without starlight, the silver leaves will fall from the Friendship Tree." Goldie explained. "And without its leaves, it will lose its magic."

The girls were horrified.

"But doesn't that mean..." Jess began.

Goldie nodded sadly. "You wouldn't be able to come back to Friendship Forest ever again."

CHAPTER FOUR

Shadow Spell

Grizelda gave a wicked laugh. "You interfering girls had better go home before the last leaf on the Friendship Tree falls," she said scornfully, "or you'll be stuck here forever!"

Lily and Jess glanced at each other. The thought of never seeing their animal friends again was awful, but so was never being able to go home.

"Oh, Goldie," said Lily with a sob. "We have to go! We couldn't leave our families."

"Yes, go!" sneered Grizelda. "Go away! No more meddling in my plans. Ha haaa!"

She snapped her fingers and disappeared in a burst of smelly yellow sparks.

"I can't imagine never coming to Friendship Forest again," Lily said. Tears filled her eyes. "We'd miss you so much!"

Jess put an arm around Lily. She felt like

crying too. "How long do you think we have before the Friendship Tree loses its magic?" she asked.

Goldie looked up at the fading stars. "The last leaf will fall when the last star fades from the sky," she said grimly.

Jess and Lily looked up.

"We have to try and stop Grizelda's plan," said Jess determinedly. "If only we could get the Fuzzybrushes and the moonstone back…they could dance and bring out the stars again. Then we can stay here."

"Where should we start looking?" Lily asked Goldie.

But the cat was staring at the lighthouse. Her green eyes had narrowed and her tail twitched thoughtfully.

"What is it, Goldie?" asked Lily. "Have you seen something?"

Goldie pointed at the lighthouse wall.

"Look at those funny shadows," she said. "I can't see what's casting them."

Ruby gave a squeal. "One of them's waving!" she cried.

They peered closer.

"Each shadow has two pointy ears," said Lily.

"And a bushy tail," Jess added. "Oh, my goodness, they're—"

"Foxes!" cried Goldie. "Smudge has turned the Fuzzybrushes into shadows!"

Ruby ran over to the lighthouse and tried to hug one of the shadow foxes, but she couldn't.

Lily put her arm around Ruby and kissed the top of her head. "Don't worry," she said. "We'll make Smudge reverse his magic and give us the moonstone. You'll get your family back."

Ruby wiped her eyes with her tail. "And then we'll bring out the stars again," she said firmly.

Jess tickled the cub's fluffy ears. "You're a very brave little fox," she said.

Goldie had been thinking. "I wonder," she said, "if any of the night-time animals are in Toadstool Glade. Maybe someone's seen where Smudge went."

"We have to hurry," Lily said. As she stared up at the sky, one star blinked out, then another.

The forest was so much quieter than when all the animals were awake. A few of the little cottages they passed still had lights on in the windows, but most of them were dark.

"Look!" Lily pointed to the Toadstool café. A light was shining from the window. Lily, Jess, Goldie and Ruby rushed over to peek inside. Lucy Longwhiskers the rabbit and her dad waved to them from the window, then came out to see them. Lucy was wearing spotty pink pyjamas and

fluffy rabbit slippers.

"Lucy couldn't sleep, so I was just making her some hot chocolate," Mr Longwhiskers explained. "Would you like some too?"

"I'm afraid we haven't got time," said Goldie. She quickly explained what had happened.

The rabbits were shocked.

"Poor you," Lucy said, hugging Ruby. "You must be so worried."

"I am," said the fox cub, "we have to find Smudge. Have you seen him?"

The rabbits sadly shook their heads.

But then Mr Longwhiskers hopped up and down excitedly. "You could go to the Midnight Market," he suggested.

"What's the Midnight Market?" asked Jess curiously.

"I know!" Ruby scampered off. "I'll tell you on the way!"

"Thank you!" the girls and Goldie called to the Longwhiskers as they raced after Ruby.

"The Midnight Market is where all the night-time animals buy things," Goldie explained. "I don't know why we didn't think of it before!"

"Rusty and I always buy star cookies at the market," said Ruby, as they passed the Friendship Tree. "We could get some for him. Star cookies are his favourite treat," she added sadly.

Goldie hugged her. "That's a lovely idea," she said.

As they passed the Friendship Tree, Lily caught sight of a silver pile on the ground. "What's that?" she wondered out loud.

Goldie gave a gasp. "Leaves!"

Lily and Jess glanced at each other in dismay. The Friendship Tree's lower branches were already drooping, and the silver leaves were fading to a pale, ghostly grey. As they watched, another one fluttered down to the ground.

Lily shuddered. "Come on," she said bravely. "We have to hurry! If we don't find that dragon soon, the Friendship Tree will lose its magic for ever!"

CHAPTER FIVE

The Midnight Market

Ruby bounded through the dark forest and stopped at a tall oak tree. "We're here!" the fox cub said happily. "The Midnight Market!"

"But where is it?" Lily asked, looking around in amazement. She could hear lots of voices, but she couldn't see anyone!

"Look up!" Ruby pointed her paw. Way above them, high in the trees, was a huge circular platform.

Jess peered around the tree trunks. It was getting darker and darker as one by one the stars faded. Suddenly she remembered her torch. She pulled it out of her pocket and switched it on. "How do we get up there?" she asked, swinging her torch around. "I can't see a staircase or a ladder."

Ruby grinned. "I'll show you!" She led them to a wooden platform on the ground beneath the middle tree. It had a

fence around the edge with a gate.

A thick loop of vine hung beside it.

"It's a lift!" said Jess.

Ruby opened the gate and they all got onto the lift. Then Ruby darted over to the vine, tugged it, and up they went! Up and up, until the lift stopped at a wide wooden walkway that stretched across the treetops.

The Midnight Market!

In the middle of the platform there were tables laden with fruit tarts, strawberry toffees, bobble hats, mossy headbands and necklaces made of nuts and seeds. The market was decorated with vines covered in berries that hung on the edges of the tables and around

the branches. But instead of enjoying themselves, the animals at the market were huddled together, talking in worried voices.

"We're too frightened to fly high," trilled a nightingale, "ever since we heard that there's a shadow dragon about."

"Everybody must leap a cookout," said a familiar voice. "I mean keep a lookout." It was their friend Mr Cleverfeather the owl, getting his words muddled as usual!

The girls hurried over to him. All the other animals clustered around.

"Hello, Goldie. Hello, Jess and Lily," said Mr Silverback the badger. "And who's that? Oh, it's little Ruby Fuzzybrush!"

Mr Cleverfeather introduced the girls to the animals they hadn't met before. The nightingale, who was called Melody Sweetsong, trilled a musical greeting. A little pair of bats called Luna and

Dusky Longears fluttered round them with their soft velvety wings, squeaking, "Helloelloello!"

Mr Cleverfeather waved a wing at a family of brown owls. "These are my cousins, the Wisefeathers."

"Hoo hoo," they said. "We've heard about yoohoo!"

"And this," Mr Cleverfeather said, "is Dora Tinytail."

At first, Jess and Lily couldn't see Dora,

but they lowered their torches and, in the yellow glow, saw the most adorable little golden dormouse.

When Jess put her hand down, Dora climbed on to it and curled up, with her fluffy tail wrapped around her. She yawned and immediately fell asleep.

"She's so cute!" said Lily.

"She should try to stay awake," said Mr Silverback, "in case that dragon appears."

"And what has happened to the light night and the tars – I mean, the nightlight and the stars?" Mr Cleverfeather asked.

Goldie explained about the poor Fuzzybrushes and the star dance, and how they badly needed to make Smudge reverse his spell. "Have any of you seen him?" she asked.

Everyone shook their heads. "The problem is," said Mr Silverback, "that even us night-time animals would have trouble spotting Smudge when it's this dark."

"I'm not surprised," said Jess, glancing up at the sky. There were only a few stars left. "I can hardly see a thing now, even with a torch. How can we search the whole forest?"

All the animals looked at each other anxiously.

"What about fireflies?" Jess exclaimed, "They helped us before."

"They live too far away," Goldie said.

"I think I've got just the thing," Mr Cleverfeather told them. "Some lightbites I was making for a party."

"Lightbites?" Jess said in confusion.

"I mean bright lights," Mr Cleverfeather said, shaking his head.

"Those sounds perfect!" Lily gasped.

"But they're all the way over at my workshop," Mr Cleverfeather sighed.

"Yoohoo start looking, and we'll fly and get them," Mrs Wisefeather volunteered. "Then we'll come and find yoohoo!" The brown owls flapped their wings and sped off.

"They won't be back soon enough," Goldie looked worried as another star disappeared.

"But we have to find Smudge!" Ruby cried, leaning against a tree trunk and cuddling her tail sadly.

As she looked at the tiny fox, Jess gave a cry. "Ruby, look at your tail!"

The fox cub shook her tail. Black dust came off.

Lily put her hand against the tree trunk. It was covered in soot!

"Look!" Lily cried. "I know how to find Smudge! All we have to do is follow the trail of soot!"

"There's more over hereherehere!" called Luna Longears.

Mr Cleverfeather pointed a wing.

"Wish they, everyone – I mean, this way! Keep looking for the soot!"

Lily and Jess shone their torches ahead. The narrow beams didn't show much, but with all the night-time animals working together, they were finding the trail.

Jess could hear Ruby's footsteps as the little cub scampered along beside them.

"We don't want anyone to let gost – I mean, get lost," said Mr Cleverfeather. "Goldie, hold my wingtip. Jess, you hold her paw, and Lily can hold Jess's arm. Ruby, you hold onto Lily."

All the night-time animals held onto

each other as they walked carefully through the forest.

Occasionally one of the animals called out as they spotted some soot on a tree branch or bush where Smudge had

bumped his way along.

It got darker and darker as the stars went out one by one. The animals huddled together, trying to search by the light of the girls' torches.

Finally they spotted a faint glow ahead. "Is it the Wisefeathers with the lights?" Goldie asked.

"No! That's the moonstone!" Ruby cried, racing forward.

"Quick!" cried Lily.

The girls rushed after her, into the shadowy darkness of the forest. Jess's foot caught a fallen branch, and she tripped.

"Ow!" she cried.

"Are you OK?" asked Lily, stopping to help her up.

"I'm fine," Jess said.

Suddenly there was a chuckle in the tree next to them. The girls swung around, shining their torches towards the noise. There, wrapped around the trunk, was Smudge the dragon!

Smudge gave another laugh. "Hee, hee! Nice darkness makes everyone else fall over too!" Then he scrambled inside a hollow in a tree trunk, taking the moonstone with him.

Lily turned to Jess in excitement. "So that's why Smudge likes the dark so much," she said. "In the dark, he's not the only one who's clumsy!"

"If we can show him how to stop tripping over all the time, maybe he'll lift the spell on the Fuzzybrushes," Jess said.

"Great idea!" said Lily. "The stars will come back and the Friendship Tree will be safe. We just need to work out how to teach a dragon not to be clumsy…"

CHAPTER SIX

Ruby's Dance

After Lily and Jess had told the others their idea, Goldie's whiskers drooped. "It's a great plan, girls," she said, "but how will we stop Smudge tripping over? I can't think of anything."

Ruby jumped up and down excitedly. "But I can!" she cried.

"What's your plan, Ruby?" asked Lily.

Ruby swished her tail. "Remember the star dance we showed you?"

The girls and Goldie nodded.

"When Rusty and I first started learning it, our tails got in the way," Ruby said. "But once we'd learned some dance moves, we stopped tripping over them. Dancing's really good for learning how to keep your balance, you see," she added.

Jess grinned – she'd guessed what Ruby was thinking. "So if you teach Smudge some dance moves, he'll be less clumsy!"

"And then he won't want to be in the dark any more, as he won't be tripping over all the time," Goldie finished. She reached over and hugged the little cub. "That's brilliant, Ruby!"

"Smudge!" Lily called up at the tree where the dragon was hiding.

Smudge's voice echoed from inside the tree. "Go away!" he grumbled.

"Ruby's going to teach us how to dance," Jess called back. "Why don't you come and join in with us?"

"No!" Smudge. "I'm staying in here."

Ruby looked disappointed, and Lily felt a nervous swirling in her tummy. They had to make Smudge reverse his spell, or the Friendship Tree would lose its magic and the Fuzzybrushes would be shadows forever!

Just then there was a flapping sound and the Wisefeather owls appeared, carrying a long string of beautiful lights in their beaks. The owls perched on the nearby trees and Lily and Jess blinked up at them happily. The golden bright lights twinkled above them like tiny chandeliers.

"Come on, let's make Smudge change his mind!" Jess said determinedly. "Everyone, make some music!"

The night-time animals gathered in a circle, lit by the golden lights. Melody Sweetsong the nightingale started to sing. Mr Silverback clapped his paws while the Longears bat family whistled.

Ruby's pointy ears pricked up happily. She held onto her tail with one paw and skipped in a circle. Goldie held her tail and followed after her, while the girls pretended to hold tails too and skipped along after them.

"Now hop like this!" Ruby called. She jumped from right to left, waving her tail in the opposite direction. Goldie and the girls copied her, the girls waving a hand instead of a tail. They were all grinning.

"This is so much fun!" cried Jess.

Lily giggled as Ruby started shuffling backwards, wiggling her paws in front of her. As she copied the fox cub, she saw Smudge peeking out of the hollow in his tree. He was bobbing his head in time to the music.

"Let's keep going," Lily whispered.

"I think it's working!"

Ruby led them in a waltz around Smudge's tree. Every few beats, she paused to kick out a paw and shimmy her tail.

Jess was last in line, and a movement from behind caught her eye.

It was Smudge! He was skipping after them, flapping his wings and dancing!

"Hee!" laughed Smudge, clapping his scaly paws. "Look at me!"

"Hooray!" cried Lily.

They all gathered around the dancing dragon. Ruby took his paw in hers. "Hold your tail in your other paw, like this," she said, showing him, "then hop from foot to foot!"

"Whee!" said Smudge, doing as Ruby said. He finished the move with a flap of his wings and a wiggle of his head.

Goldie clapped. "That's great, Smudge! You're a really good dancer!"

Just then Smudge tripped over his tail. Jess held her breath. If Smudge didn't manage to dance, he might not help the Fuzzybrushes!

But to their relief the dragon wobbled, then turned it into a twirling dance move!

"Well done, Smudge!" Ruby cried.

Jess pointed up at the glittering lights. "We couldn't dance without Mr Cleverfeather's bright lights, though," she said. "We wouldn't be able to see what we're doing. Smudge, will you lift the spell you put on the Fuzzybrushes? Then you can dance under the stars every night."

Smudge nodded his scaly head. "I want everyone to see me now," he said. "Yes, I'll take away the spell!"

Ruby gave a cry of delight. "I'll have

my family back!" she cried.

"And the Friendship Tree will be safe," said Jess, smiling. "Lily and I can keep coming to the forest!"

CHAPTER SEVEN

Starlight

The Wisefeathers flapped through the forest, holding the bright lights to guide the way. Smudge flew along beside them, carrying the magical moonstone. When his tail got in the way of his legs, he turned his stumble into a dance move, hopping and waving his paws.

"Go, Smudge!" cheered Jess.

But a dreadful shock awaited the group as they passed the Friendship Tree.

"There are barely any leaves left!" Jess gasped. "We're running out of time!"

They raced to the lighthouse, where three fox shadows stood waiting.

"Don't worry, Mum, we're going to take the spell off you," Ruby said.

The two big shadows reached out to the little cub, but stopped when Smudge skipped towards them.

"It's OK," Lily told them. "Smudge is going to free you."

With a final hop, Smudge huffed a dark sooty cloud over the three shadows. It swirled around them then, with a puff, it was gone and there stood Mr and Mrs Fuzzybrush and little Rusty!

The whole fox family hugged each other, rolling over and over in a jumble of legs and fluffy tails.

Finally, they got to their feet. Their ears pricked up as Goldie told them about their adventure.

"Thank you for saving us," said Mrs Fuzzybrush, "and for looking after Ruby."

"She's a very good dance teacher," said Jess. "We couldn't have done it without her!"

Ruby hugged the girls and Goldie. "It was a brilliant adventure," she said, "but I was a bit scared."

Mr Fuzzybrush kissed her nose. "Scared? You?" he said. "No other fox cub has ever been brave enough to teach a dragon how to dance!"

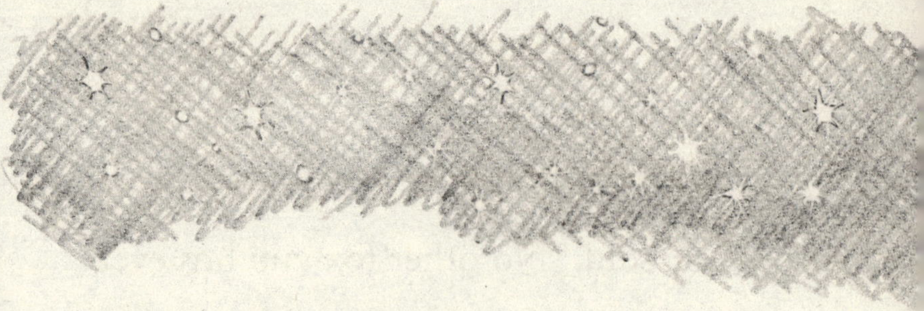

"Speaking of dancing, can you do your star dance, please?" Jess said, looking up at the sky.

There was just one little star left.

"Hurry," begged Lily, thinking of the leaves on the Friendship Tree.

Everyone ran into the clearing. Smudge put the moonstone in the middle and, as

the girls and Goldie watched, the foxes began their stepping, gliding, twirling dance. Smudge sat nearby, swishing his tail in time. As the tips of the foxes' bushy tails touched, the moonstone began to glow.

"There!" said Jess, pointing up at the inky sky. A star was twinkling. More and more appeared, and soon the sky was

dusted with sparkling starlight.

"Perfect for dancing under!" said Smudge, clapping his paws as he gazed up at the twinkling stars.

As the moonstone shone brighter than ever before, the Fuzzybrushes finished and took a bow. The star dance was complete.

"That looked so magical!" said Jess.

"It *was* magical!" said Lily. "Now the Friendship Tree will be safe."

Ruby was whispering to her parents. They nodded, and she went to stand

close to where the black shadow dragon was perched.

"Smudge, would you like to learn some more dance moves?" she asked.

"Oh, yes!" Smudge cried.

"Then my mum and dad say that you can come and stay at the lighthouse with us," Ruby said, "as long as you promise not make everything too sooty."

Smudge flew in a big loop-the-loop, got tangled in his tail, turned it into a hop through the air, and landed in front of the Fuzzybrushes. "Thank you!" he said happily. "I'll be good, I promise!"

Ruby, Rusty and Smudge held paws and twirled around the moonstone.

Lily and Jess grinned at each other, then ran to join in, followed by the other night-time animals. They all danced happily under the twinkling stars.

Finally it was time for the girls to go home. They hugged Ruby and her family goodbye, and gave Smudge a hug too.

As they walked happily back through the forest, Jess turned to Lily and Goldie, "Have you noticed that Grizelda's dragons don't seem to like helping her very much?" she said.

Goldie nodded. "Perhaps Grizelda forced them to be her servants."

"I feel sorry for them," said Lily.

Jess agreed.

"Maybe we should find a way to send them back to wherever they came from," she suggested.

"Do you think we could?" asked Lily. "Oh! Look at the Friendship Tree."

New silver leaves were already appearing on the branches, sparkling in the starlight.

"I'm so glad the tree is safe," said Lily. "Imagine never being able to visit Friendship Forest again!"

Goldie touched a paw to the trunk, and a door appeared. "I'm so happy you girls can still come here," said Goldie.

"I don't know what we'd do without you! Grizelda still has one more dragon, and she's bound to cause more trouble soon!"

Lily hugged her. "Whatever she does next, we'll stop her."

"I know you will," said Goldie.

The girls stepped through the door, into the golden light. The tingle began, and they knew they were growing back to their proper size.

As the glow faded, Jess and Lily found themselves back in Brightley Meadow. By the light of their torches, they crossed the stream back to the wildlife hospital.

Jess yawned as they walked up the garden. "I know no time passes while we're in Friendship Forest," she said, "but after that adventure I'm sleepy!"

"Let's check the fox cubs," said Lily, shining her torch into the run. Four amber eyes stared back at her, then the cubs carried on chasing each other around and around.

"They look like they're dancing!" said Jess with a laugh.

"Just like the Fuzzybrushes!" Lily looked at her best friend and grinned.

The girls linked arms as they walked

home. What magic would they see on their next adventure in Friendship Forest? They couldn't wait to find out!

The End

Grizelda's dragons are causing more trouble in Friendship Forest! Can Jess, Lily, Goldie and little Rosie Gigglepip stop Breezy's terrible storm in the next adventure,

Rosie Gigglepip's Lucky Escape

Turn over for a sneak peek . . .

Friendship Forest was usually filled with warmth and sunshine, but today it looked completely different. The tree branches thrashed about wildly in a fierce wind and leaves and petals swirled through the air. Rain poured down, splashing in puddles everywhere.

"What's happening?" Lily cried, her dark hair whipping around her face.

"It's a storm!" cried Goldie, over the howling wind. "I've never seen one as bad as this!"

Now that they were in the forest, Goldie could talk to them at last. She stood upright beside the girls, almost up to their shoulders, one paw holding her glittery scarf so it couldn't be snatched away by the wind.

As they huddled against the tree trunk, Jess turned to their friend. "Goldie," she cried in alarm, "what's wrong with Friendship Forest?"

Read

Rosie Gigglepip's Lucky Escape

to find out what happens next!

Magic Animal Friends

Read all the Magic Animal Friends adventures and be part of the secret!

Series Two

OUT NOW!
Look out for
Jess and Lily's
next adventure –
Amelia Sparklepaw's Party
Problem!

3 stories in 1!

www.magicanimalfriends.com

Puzzle Fun!

Can you match Ruby Fuzzybrush to the correct shadow? Do you know who the other shadows belong to?

A)

B)

C)

ANSWERS

A) Poppy Muddlepup
B) Sophie Flufftail
C) Ruby Fuzzybrush

Jess and Lily's Animal Facts

Lily and Jess love lots of different animals – both in Friendship Forest and in the real world.

Here are their top facts about

FOXES

like Ruby Fuzzybrush

- A fox's tail is called a 'brush'.
- A female fox is called a 'vixen'.
- Foxes will eat almost anything from berries and worms to sausages and jam sandwiches!
- Foxes have very good hearing and are very fast. Some can run at 30 miles per hour!
- Foxes can jump very high and have been known to climb fences and trees.
- They also have whiskers on their legs as well as their faces. These extra whiskers help them find their way in the dark.

If you like
Magic Animal Friends,
you'll love...

ANIMAL ARK

Welcome to Animal Ark!

Animal-mad Amelia is sad about moving house, until she discovers Animal Ark, where vets look after all kinds of animals in need.

Join Amelia and her friend Sam for a brand-new series of animal adventures!